OTTO'S
LUNCHBOX

Damian Harvey
Illustrated by
Amanda Montgomery-Higham

Once there was a giant called Otto.
Every day, Otto packed his lunchbox.
Then he went to work.

The other people packed their lunchboxes too.
Then they went to work.

Otto was big and strong.
He worked hard, and the people liked him.
But there was one thing they did not like.

Every day at lunch, Otto went off alone.
He ate his lunch by himself.

The people asked, "Why does Otto go off
alone at lunch?
Why won't he eat with us?
What is in Otto's lunchbox?"

The people said, "The next time Otto goes off, let's go too."
The next day, Otto went off alone at lunch.
The people went too.

Otto opened his lunchbox.
He began to eat his food.
No one could see what Otto was eating.
But they could hear him.

"Now I will eat your hat!" Otto said.
The people saw Otto take a big bite.
CRUNCH!
Everyone could hear Otto crunching.

"Now I will eat your shoes!" Otto said.
He took an even bigger bite.
CRUNCH!

"Otto eats people!" a man called out.
"We must stop him!"
"Now I will eat you!" Otto said.
He was about to take a very big bite...

"Stop!" the people called.
"You must not eat people!"
Otto turned red.
The people looked at Otto's food.
Otto was eating a gingerbread man!

"It's bigger than my gingerbread man,"
a man said.
"Do you eat gingerbread men?" Otto asked.
"Oh, yes!" everyone said.

"Otto, why do you eat lunch all alone?"
asked a man.
"Why won't you eat with us?"

"I am a big, strong giant," Otto said.
"But I eat gingerbread men."
"Everyone can eat gingerbread men,"
the people said.
"Even big, strong giants can eat them!"

After that, Otto ate lunch with the other people — well, most of the time!